JUNE "JOE" BOYD

Fantasy Fairytales

This is a work of fiction. All of the characters, names, incidents, organizations, and dialogue in this novel are either the products of the author's imagination or are used fictitiously.

Archway Publishing books may be ordered through booksellers or by contacting:

Archway Publishing
1663 Liberty Drive
Bloomington, IN 47403
www.archwaypublishing.com
844-669-3957

Because of the dynamic nature of the Internet, any web addresses or links contained in this book may have changed since publication and may no longer be valid. The views expressed in this work are solely those of the author and do not necessarily reflect the views of the publisher, and the publisher hereby disclaims any responsibility for them.

ISBN: 978-1-6657-3244-4 (sc)
ISBN: 978-1-6657-3242-0 (hc)
ISBN: 978-1-6657-3243-7 (e)

Print information available on the last page.

Archway Publishing rev. date: 11/02/2022

One night while _____ was tucked away quietly in her bed counting down every second for her favorite stories to be read she pulls her blankets way up high, nestled under her chin waiting for grandma _____ Fairyland of stories to begin. Mommy opens up her door and turns the lights down low, then she pulls up her rocking chair and _____ face begins to glow. Mommy opens up Grandma _____ magical book and it lights up the whole room, and they drift off into a magical night.

4

It was December 24th Christmas Eve _____ and her Mommy were snuggled together by the tree, _ was waiting for what she wanted to see. She wanted to see if it was the little fat man in the red suit that was as jolly as he could be. _____ and her Mommy sit snuggled up real tight. After drinking their hot chocolate, they turned down the lights.

Outside it was snowing Christmas lights were everywhere, people were out caroling, and children were throwing snowballs in the air. Finally, the streets were quiet, everyone was nestled in their beds. Even _____ was fast asleep, with sugar plums in her head, Mommy was standing at the window and at a distance far away she could see the lights and the little reindeer, Santa, and his sleigh.

She knew he would be here soon so Mommy went to the door hoping he wouldn't see. Much to her surprise, when she saw that bright light it was Rudolph's nose shining in the moonlight she could hear the bells ringing and Santas HoHoHo's Saying Merry Christmas to everyone he knows.

So Mommy went upstairs because she wanted to see if _____was sleeping, then she finished wrapping everything that went under the tree. As Santa got closer, Mommy could hear the bells getting louder, Santa was on his way. So Mommy ran to the kitchen to get out the cookies and of course, so milk too! Then she dashes off to bed in her sheets of silk. Little did she know and she didn't see that _____ wasn't sleeping and she was being as quiet as she could be.

Mommy didn't see that _ had snuck out of bed, for she wanted to see if that jolly old man was what he was cracked up to be.
She had snuck out of her room down by the stairs and sat down on the floor waiting for Jolly St. Nick to be there, she waited for Santa for quite awhile that poor little girl, but she still had on a smile.

All of the sudden something came down from above, then dropped down through the chimney in such a roar that her eyes got real big and she wasn't tired anymore. That's when she saw this man called Santa Clause then all of a sudden Santa was walking her way and _____ tried to hide, but it was too late!

She was looking at him, and he looked up at her then _____ She looked all around because she thought she saw Santa give her a wink! He then headed towards the chimney in such a roar that the house was shaking and then the rumbling of the doors. _____ was so excited that she rushed up the stairs to her bed never telling her mom what she saw.

One day while _____ was out playing in her yard, running around laughing she was such a little card. Jumping up and down as happy as she could be then all of the sudden she saw something over around the tree so _she ran over so she could get a peek, then around the tree he did sneak.

So _____ ran around the tree and said "What could this be?" "Well I'm the Easter Bunny," the little rabbit said to me. So she asked the Easter Bunny "What is it that you do? Well, I bring you colored eggs and candy; look around, I put them all there for you.

The Easter Bunny pointed towards the yard and there were colored eggs everywhere purple orange red-yellow-green and blue. Every color you could think of I put them there just for you. _____ was so excited she ran over to see how many eggs she could find? So she ran in the house to get a basket and filled it as high as she could so could see and by the time the day was over her little basket, it was full.

Full of pretty eggs and candy and it was filled to the very top. When there were no more eggs to be found and Isabella was all done she turned around to look behind her and the Easter Bunny was gone.

One night while _____ was sleeping tucked in her bed so tight Mommy had just finished reading Grandma _____ bedtime stories for the night. She gave her good night hugs and kisses then she shut her door real tight. _____ just lay there snuggled in her blankets as snug as she could be.

Then suddenly from out of nowhere, a light, bright as it could be landed on her window sill and just sit there, as still as it could be.

_____ raised her head over her blankets, so she could take a peek then she climbed out of bed and over to the window she did sneak _____ stood there quietly looking in disbelief much to her surprise, it was the tooth fairy, and _____ sighed in relief.

Her wings were fluttering in the wind, and _____ stood there smiling and the tooth fairy looked at her and grinned. So _____ opened up her window and the tooth fairy flew right in. And she landed on my pillow and looked at me again.

Her face was sparkling with glitter and her hair was golden brown. She was a pretty little girl with wings, so as the story Isabella told.

She carried a shiny little purse, that was glittery as could be, and she carried shiny little coins. She put one under my pillow for me.

11

Once upon a time, there was this little girl named _____ lived with her Mommy and Daddy in a cabin at the edge of the woods. It was wintertime and it was starting to snow for the first time this year. _____ was so excited, it is her favorite time of year. It was starting to snow really hard and it was sticking to the ground quickly.

She hurried into the kitchen to get her Mommy. Mommy, Mommy there's a lot of snow on the ground. Can I go outside now? Yes _____ you can go outside now. _____ took off running up the stairs to her room to get her coat, scarf, hat, and gloves so Mommy could help her bundle up.

After she's finished she tells _____ if it gets too cold you know to come back in and warm up for a while then you can go back out. Okay Mommy I will and she runs out the back door. Isabella was running around laughing and jumping when all of the sudden she heard screaming. It sounded like a couple of kids screaming for help. So the screaming sounded like it was coming from the woods. _____ knows she's not supposed to go in the woods, especially all by himself.

She didn't know what to do, if she ran in to get her Mommy it could be too late. So she had to make up her mind quickly. So she took off running into the woods. She ran and ran so fast she didn't even know where she was going but she knew she had to help save them. Then the screaming stopped so_____ stopped running. She looked around and noticed her path had covered up from more snow and she was lost.

Then the screaming started again. _____ was looking around and noticed a cabin and there was smoke coming from the chimney. _____ ran to the cabin and she was about to knock on the door when she heard the screams again but this time there was an old lady's voice talking back. The children were screaming witch and the old lady said don't worry it won't take that much longer and it will all be over with.

Isabella hid at the side of the cabin she noticed a window so she snuck over to the window and peaked in. The children started screaming again. Oh no she said the witch has them in 2 pots a girl in one and a boy in the other one. So she was trying to think of a way to save the boy and girl. She wanted to run home and get Mommy to help.

She knew that would take too long and she had to act fast. So _____ needed to make a plan quickly before it was too late. So she decided to throw snowballs at the front door and when the witch runs out to see what's going on I will run in the door, shut it and lock it behind me and grab the children. Isabella started throwing the snowballs at the cabin. Then all of a sudden the front door flew open. It was the witch.

Just as she thought the witch ran out and _____ ran really fast into the cabin; she slammed the door and locked it; she then ran over to the pots and helped the children get out, then all of the sudden the door flew open it was the witch she just kicked the door in. _____ started screaming and told them to follow her. They ran so fast they didn't see where they were.

Finally after running so fast when they thought they were far enough from the witches' cabin they stopped. _____ looked at the children and asked what their names were. The little boy said my name is Hansel and the little girl said my name is Gretel. Well, she said my name is _____. I heard you screaming so I came to help you. Why was the witch cooking you in a pot? Well said Gretel she was going to make us soup. Oh, no said _____ I'm glad I came to help you but the snow was coming down so hard it covered my path and now I'm lost.

Hansel said we know where you live and we see you playing outside all the time. You don't live too far from us come on _____ follow me said, Hansel. So _ followed Hansel and Gretel. They ran so fast they were at _____ house before she knew it. Hansel and Gretel both looked at _____and said thank you Isabella you saved our lives we owe you. Maybe someday we can come and play with you if your Mommy doesn't care. _____ eyes got real big, that would be awesome, said _____ . I know she won't care. Ok, they said well see you soon.

So _____ ran into the house and went upstairs to change her clothes, and Mommy never even knew she left the yard.

June Joe Boyd is an American book author and songwriter born in Linton Indiana whose work includes A Spiritual Awakening Series and the children's book Fantasy Fairytales In 2022/2023 June Joe Boyd was honored to receive the Who's Who in America Award which is limited to individuals who possess professional integrity, demonstrate outstanding achievement in their respective fields.

At an early age, June Joe Boyd set her site on writing stories and poems however through the years kept them to herself and didn't share them with anyone until 2012 when a friend encouraged her to get them published, and soon after found herself making the Top 100 List with her first book A Spiritual Awakening.

Currently, she is working on a few different projects including fiction and non-fiction including one that could be slated for a movie with a distributor already in place.

My favorite quote

To put the right word in the right place at the right time is a rare achievement...
Mark Twain

Printed in the United States
by Baker & Taylor Publisher Services